This book belongs to

..................................................................................................

ANIMATED CLASSICS

Disney

# Tim Burton's The Nightmare Before Christmas

**Acknowledgments**

Special thanks to Tim Burton and his team for their support of this book, as well as the staff at the Walt Disney Animation Research Library for their assistance and for providing the artwork for this book.



Published by Scholastic Australia in 2021.

First published in the UK in 2020 by Studio Press Books,
an imprint of Bonnier Books UK.

Scholastic Australia Pty Limited
PO Box 579 Gosford NSW 2250
ABN 11 000 614 577
www.scholastic.com.au

Part of the Scholastic Group
Sydney • Auckland • New York • Toronto • London • Mexico City • New Delhi
Hong Kong • Buenos Aires • Puerto Rico



ISBN 978-1-76120-042-7

Printed in China.

Text adapted by Sally Morgan
Edited by Frankie Jones
Designed by Nia Williams
Cover designed by Rob Ward
Cover illustrated by Chellie Carroll
Production by Emma Kidd

10 9 8 7 6 5 4 3 2 24 25 / 2

ANIMATED CLASSICS

Disney

# Tim Burton's The Nightmare Before Christmas

# It was Halloween night in Halloween Town.

Ghouls, goblins, werewolves and witches gathered in the town square to wait for the return of their leader, Jack Skellington – the pumpkin king.

Fresh from his night of fright, Jack Skellington rode into town, his fearsome pumpkin costume ablaze. The admiring crowd of monsters cheered, as Jack leapt from his wooden horse and doused the flames in a fountain.

"Great Halloween, everybody," said the two-faced Mayor.

"I believe it was our most horrible yet," added Jack Skellington.

"Thanks to you, Jack!" replied the Mayor.

Everyone in Halloween Town thought Jack Skellington was a wonderful Pumpkin King and they couldn't wait to tell him how much they adored him.

"You're such a scream, Jack!" one vampire cheered.

"You're a witch's fondest dream!" cried a witch.

From the edge of the crowd, a ragdoll named Sally watched Jack, her heart filled with longing.

Suddenly, an evil scientist, grabbed hold of Sally's arm.

"The deadly nightshade you slipped me wore off, Sally," the scientist said.

The scientist was Sally's creator, Dr Finklestein, who had created Sally in his laboratory. In return, he expected Sally to be his companion, forever.

“Let go!” Sally cried.

“You’re coming with me!” Dr Finklestein said, trying to pull Sally away.

Thinking quickly, Sally picked the threads that attached her ragdoll arm, causing her arm to detach. She fled to the graveyard, leaving her arm to knock Dr Finklestein on the head.

In the square, the crowd tried to get closer to their king. Soon, Jack found himself surrounded.

"Ooh, Jack, you make wounds ooze and flesh crawl!" cooed a swamp monster.

But none of the praise and good cheer mattered to Jack. Like Sally, he wanted to escape, too.

While the Mayor made an announcement, Jack took the opportunity to slip away.

"Nice work, Bone Daddy," a musician called after him.

"Yeah, I guess so. Just like last year," Jack replied.

Jack walked forlornly to the graveyard, where he summoned Zero from his tomb. Zero was Jack's ghost dog who had a glowing orange pumpkin nose.

As Jack walked, he boasted to Zero of his fame throughout the world as the king of fear. But, Jack was bored of making people scream all the time. He wanted more than being the pumpkin king.

Jack felt something was missing from his life. He didn't think anyone in Halloween Town could possibly understand.

But someone did understand.

Sally had heard everything from behind a gravestone. She knew exactly how Jack felt. But Sally was too timid to reveal herself, so she watched as he walked into the forest with Zero.

"Sally!" Dr Finklestein called, when he heard her return to his castle. "You've come back."

"I had to," Sally said.

"For this?" He said, holding up Sally's arm. He led her to his laboratory where he reattached her arm.

Sally told Dr Finklestein that she was feeling restless.

"It's a phase, my dear. It'll pass," Dr Finklestein said. "We need to be patient, that's all."

But Sally didn't want to be patient.

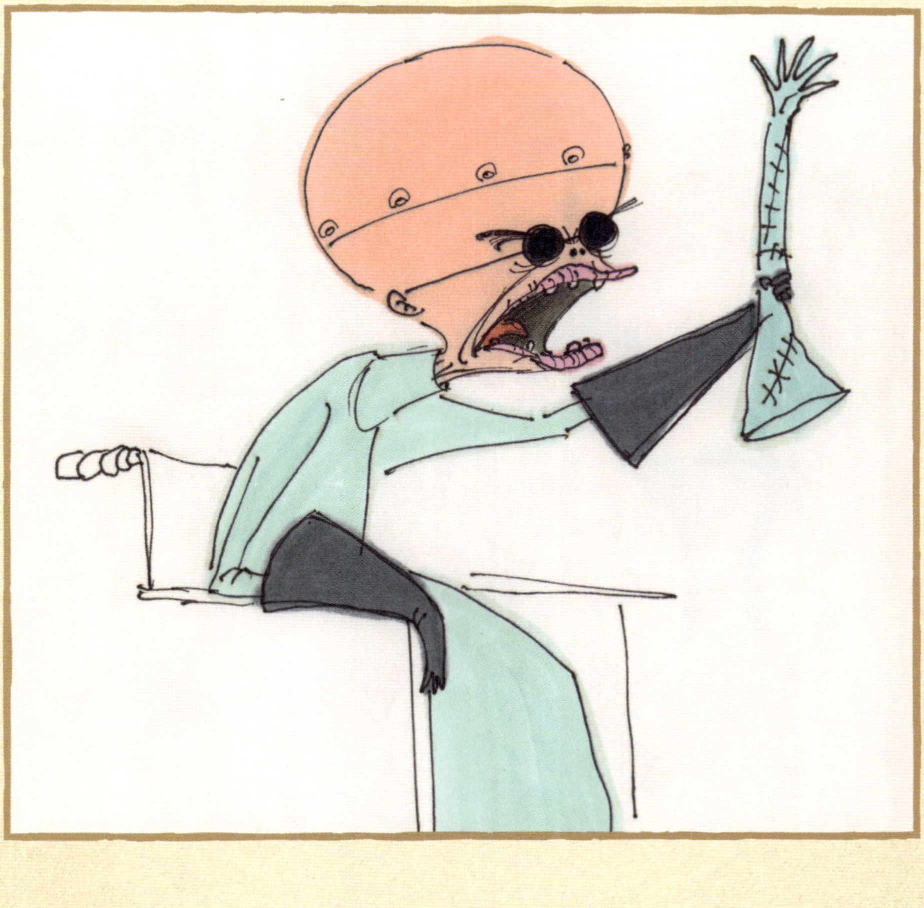

Early the next morning, the Mayor arrived at Jack's house to discuss plans for next Halloween. The Mayor climbed up the steps and rang the bell, but there was no answer. The Mayor pounded on the door, but there was still no answer.

"Jack! Answer me!" the Mayor cried. But Jack could not answer because he was not home. In fact, Jack hadn't been home all night.

At the very edge of Halloween Town, the pumpkin sun blazed above the skeletal trees of the forest. “Where are we?” Jack yawned, tired after a long night of wandering.

Jack had found himself in a place unlike any he had been to before.

“What is this?” Jack wondered, as he stepped into a clearing. All around him, stood trees with strange pictures carved into their trunks.

One was carved with a pretty egg, one with a plump turkey and another a bold red heart, but one carving stood out to Jack more than any other, that of a brightly decorated, green tree.

As Jack looked closer, he saw that the carvings were in fact doors with shining doorknobs.

Curious, Jack took hold of the doorknob on the tree door, turned it and pulled. The door opened. Jack leaned inside to see where it led.

But all he could see was darkness. Jack stepped back, disappointed, but as he did so, a flurry of snowflakes swirled out from the tree and pulled him inside. The door slammed shut behind him, leaving Zero in the forest alone.

Down Jack tumbled, as spiralling snowflakes eddied around him.

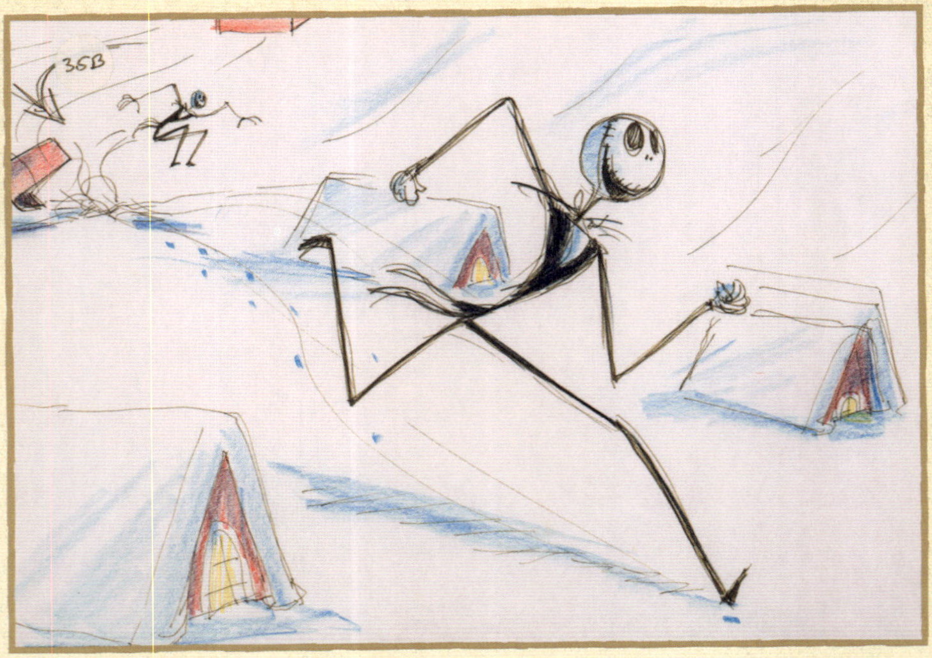


Jack landed with a thump. A bright flash blinded him for a moment. As his sight returned, Jack found himself sitting on top of a snow-covered hill, overlooking the most cheerful looking town he had ever seen.

Jack jumped up and slid down the hill towards the town.

When he arrived, Jack wondered if he was dreaming. All around him people were laughing and singing. It was nothing like dark and gloomy Halloween Town. Everything was bright and colourful. There were no monsters, no witches and nobody was scared.

Jack wanted to know more about this mysterious place. But where was he?

Not looking where he was going, Jack crashed into a signpost.

"Christmas Town?" Jack read.

Back in Halloween Town the search was on for the missing pumpkin king.

"We've got to find Jack," the Mayor declared. "Is there anywhere we've forgotten to check?"

But there wasn't.

"It's time to sound the alarms!" cried the Mayor.

High in Dr Finklestein's castle, Sally heard the alarm. Longing for her share of the excitement, she slipped deadly nightshade into her master's soup.

"Lunch!" Sally announced as she entered Dr Finklestein's lab. But something about the smell of the soup made the scientist suspicious.

"Until you taste it, I won't swallow a spoonful," he said.

Sally reached for the spoon, but knocked it to the ground. When she reached down to pick it up, she pulled a spoon filled with holes from her sock.

Sally took a big fake spoonful of soup.

"See? Scrumptious," she said, placing the bowl in front of him. Sally watched with delight as Dr Finklestein gulped it down.

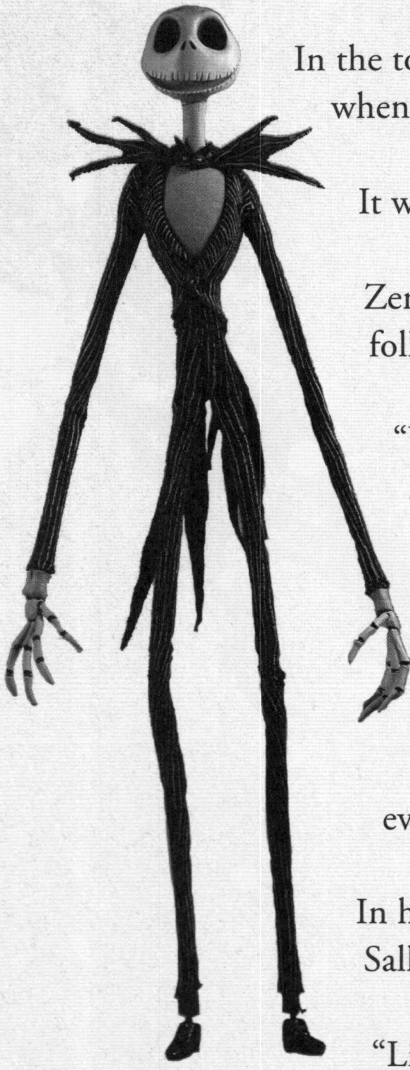

In the town square, the Mayor was out of ideas, when suddenly there was the sound of barking.

It was Zero!

Zero flew into Halloween Town, with Jack following close behind, riding a snowmobile.

"Where have you been?" demanded the Mayor, as a crowd gathered around Jack.

"Call a town meeting and I'll tell everyone all about it," replied Jack.

There was no time to waste. The Mayor immediately drove through the town to tell everyone about the meeting.

In his laboratory, Dr Finklestein slept soundly as Sally snuck out to join the meeting.

"Listen everyone," Jack said, as he strode onto the stage. "I want to tell you about Christmas Town."

Jack told everyone about what he'd seen and showed them the souvenirs he had brought back. He tried to explain the sights and the sounds and the warmth he felt when he was there.

The town loved it. They wanted to try Christmas for themselves.

They gasped at the bright lights and the presents and wondered what horrible things they could put inside.

Jack told them that Christmas was nice and not frightening. But the town didn't understand.

Unsure how to explain, Jack told them about the shadowy leader of Christmas Town. Jack had not met this ruler, but his description was vivid and terrifying. He said the people of Christmas Town, called their king, "Sandy Claws."

The crowd were delighted. But Jack knew they were still missing something.

Later, in front of the fire, Jack searched through his books for a way to better explain Christmas. He wondered if science might help.

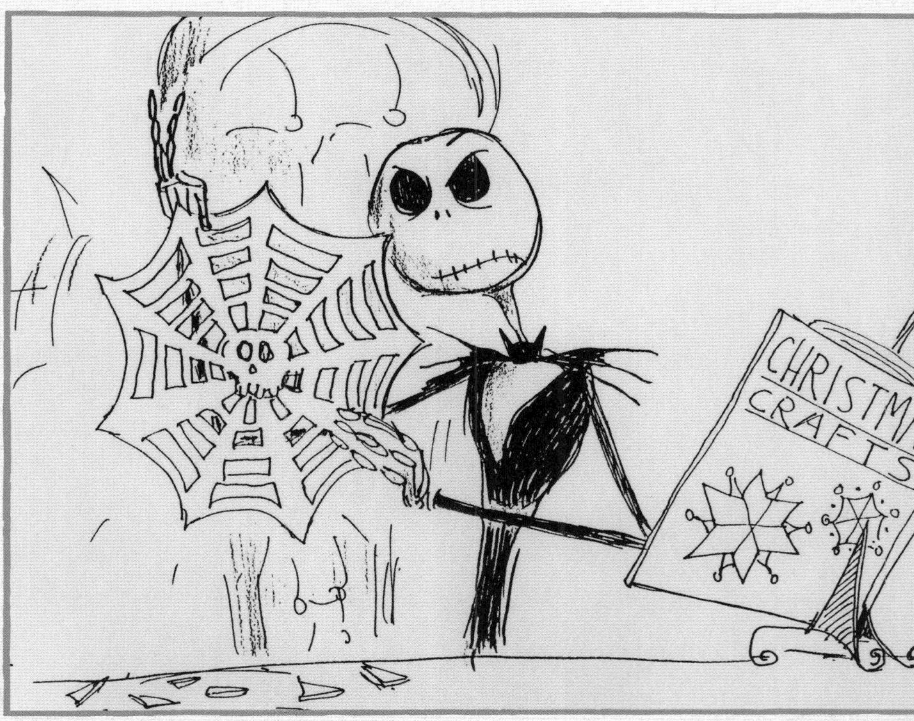

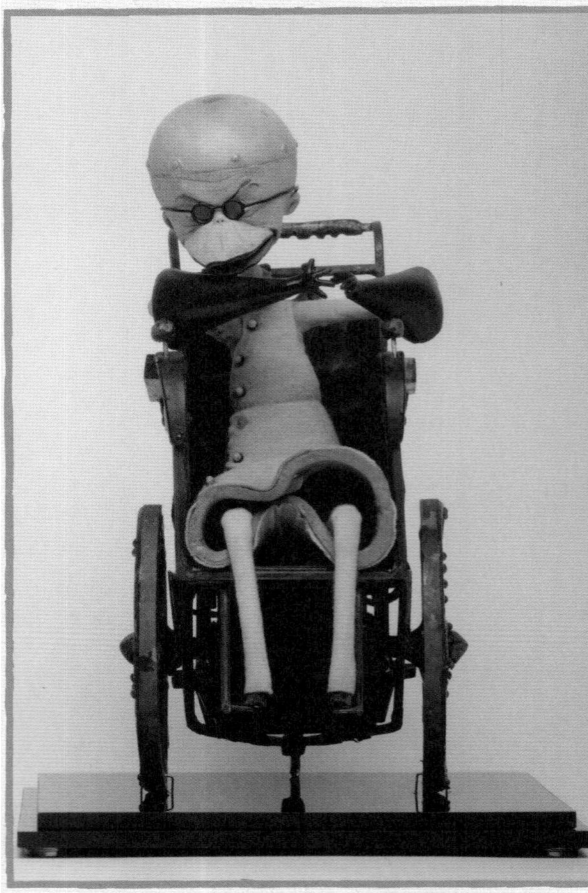

The next morning, Dr Finklestein locked Sally in a dungeon to make sure she never poisoned him again. As he secured the lock, his doorbell rang.

It was Jack.

"Doctor, I need to borrow some equipment," Jack said and explained that he wanted to do some experiments. The evil scientist gave Jack everything he needed while Sally listened.

At home, Jack crushed holly berries under a microscope, sliced open a teddy bear and boiled an ornament over a Bunsen burner. Jack made all kinds of observations, but he didn't know what they meant.

From her dungeon, Sally saw the glowing light from Jack's experiments. She decided to make him some provisions.

Unlocking the window of her cell, Sally lowered the basket of food to the ground and leapt after it. She landed with a thud, her body broken on the pavement. But all was not lost. Sally picked up her pieces and sewed herself back together.

Sally took her basket to the pumpkin king's window. Jack brought it inside, but when he looked out to thank Sally, she was gone.

Sally hid behind a wall and pulled the petals from a dead flower. She wondered if she would ever have the courage to tell Jack how she felt.

Suddenly, Sally had a terrifying vision. The flower she held in her hand turned into a Christmas tree and then burst into flames. All that remained was a charred stick.

Meanwhile, Jack had not left his house in days. The people of Halloween Town worried about their pumpkin king.

In his makeshift lab, Jack was no closer to discovering the meaning of Christmas. He was getting frustrated. Eventually, Jack decided that it didn't matter whether or not he understood the magic of Christmas, as long as he believed in it.

He believed in Christmas so much that he was sure he could improve it. Jack knew what he had to do. He threw open the window and announced, "This year, Christmas will be ours!"

But there was a lot to be done and Jack had jobs for everyone. The whole town lined up to receive their tasks.

Jack asked the vampires to make dolls and Dr Finklestein to make the reindeer.

"How horrible our Christmas will be!" cheered the Mayor.

"No, how jolly!" said Jack, correcting him.

Jack assigned his most important task to Halloween Town's best trick or treaters, Lock, Shock and Barrel. Jack wanted them to kidnap Sandy Claws.

Jack made them promise to tell no one about their mission, especially their master, Oogie Boogie.

Oogie Boogie was a mean creature so terrible that all of the ghosts, goblins, witches and werewolves were frightened of him. His body was a shapeless sack, bursting at the seams with creepy crawlies and his gaping mouth had a slithering snake for a tongue.

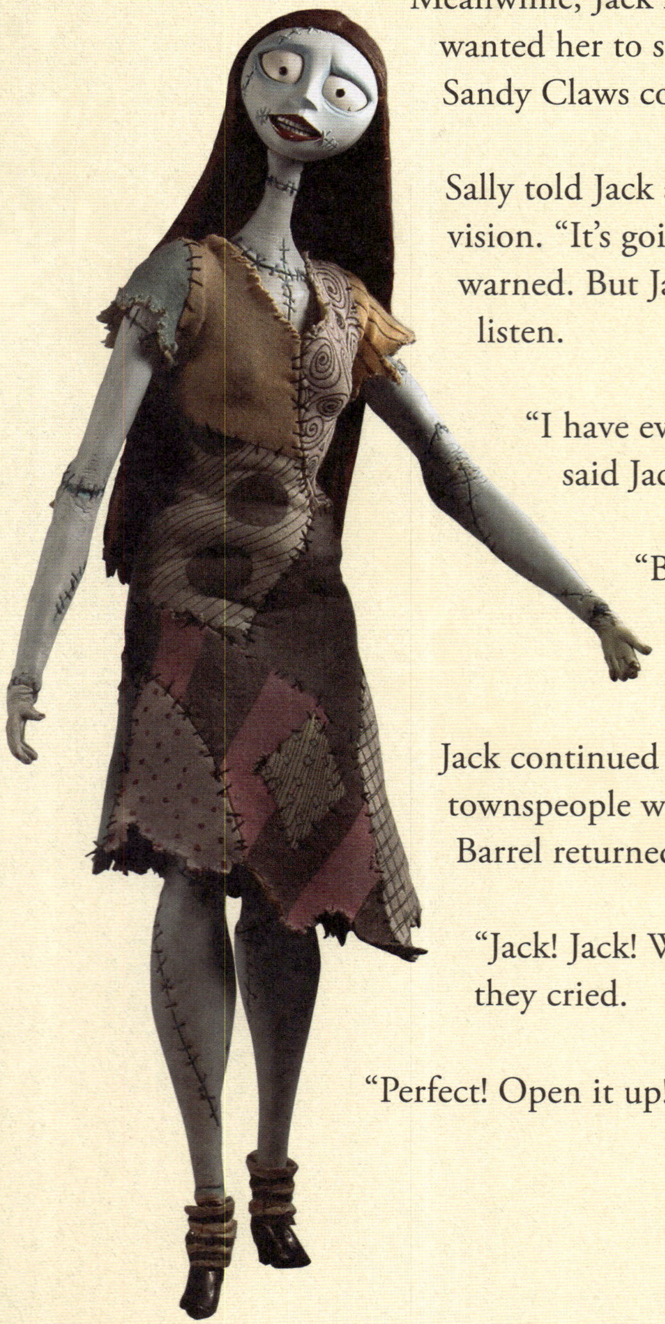

Meanwhile, Jack had a job for Sally. He wanted her to sew him his very own Sandy Claws costume.

Sally told Jack all about her terrifying vision. "It's going to be a disaster," she warned. But Jack was too excited to listen.

"I have every confidence in you," said Jack.

"But it seems wrong to me, very wrong," Sally said as she walked away.

Jack continued to hand out tasks to the townspeople when Lock, Shock and Barrel returned with a mysterious sack.

"Jack! Jack! We got him! We got him!" they cried.

"Perfect! Open it up! Quickly," Jack said.

But when they opened the sack, there was no Sandy Claws. Instead, out hopped a pink bunny, carrying a basket of eggs.

"Take him back!" Jack commanded. Jack apologised to the startled bunny and sent them on their way.

As the big day drew closer, the two worlds, Halloween Town and Christmas Town, worked hard to create their versions of Christmas. But while the toys built in Christmas Town were guaranteed to bring delight, the citizens of Halloween Town made gifts that would cause terror. Halloween Town was making Christmas the only way they knew how. They were making Christmas scary.

On Christmas Eve, everything was almost ready. Ghosts and mummies rushed to the town square with their ghoulish gifts to put in Jack's sleigh. But Jack's sleigh was not jolly and red like the one in Christmas Town. Jack's sleigh was black and built from a coffin and was to be pulled by reindeer skeletons.

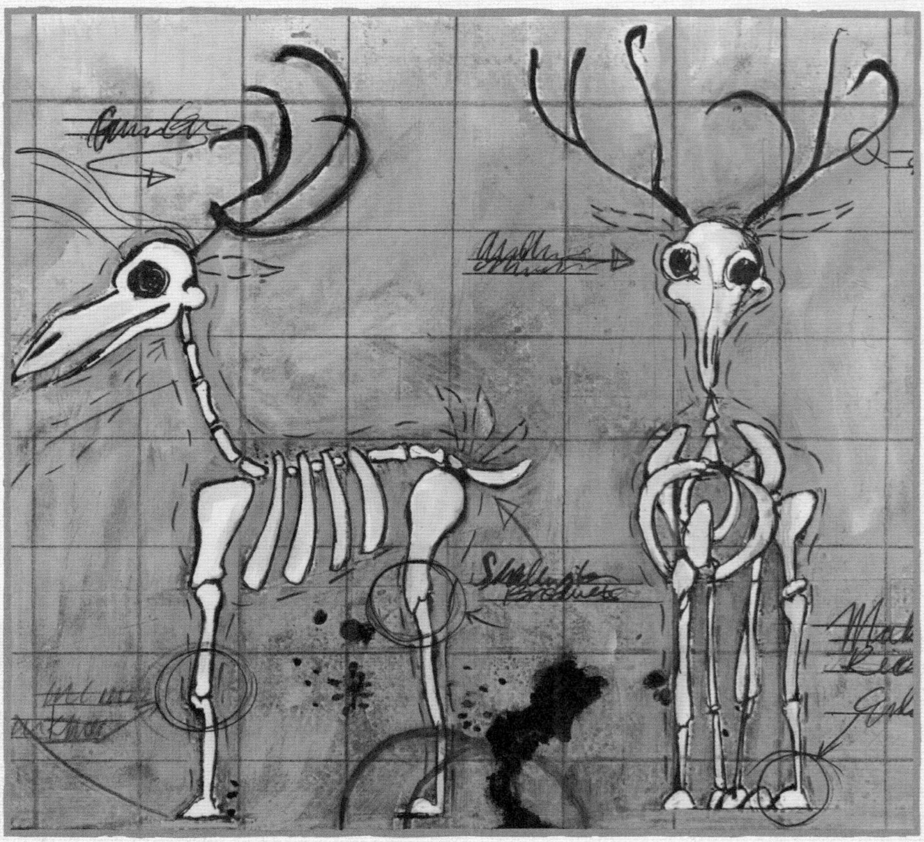

Christmas Town was almost ready, too. Santa was checking his nice and naughty list when his doorbell rang.

"Now, who could that be?" wondered Santa as he got up from his chair.

"Trick or treat!" cried Lock, Shock and Barrel on Santa's doorstep. The treacherous trick or treaters bundled Santa into a sack, threw him in their walking bathtub and raced back to Halloween Town.

Meanwhile, Sally put the finishing touches on Jack's Sandy Claws costume.

"You don't look like yourself, Jack. Not at all," she said.

"Isn't that wonderful?" cried Jack.

"Jack, I know you think something's missing, but..." Sally began.

"You're right. Something is missing. But what?" said Jack, studying his reflection.

Then he heard a cry.

"Jack! Jack! This time we bagged him!" Lock, Shock and Barrel had returned from Christmas Town. They released Sandy Claws from their sack.

"Let me out!" demanded Santa Claus.

"Why, you have hands. You don't have claws at all!" exclaimed Jack shaking Sandy Claws' hand. Santa was very confused.

"You don't need to have another worry about Christmas this year. Consider this a vacation Sandy, a reward. It's your turn to take it easy," Jack explained.

"But there must be some mistake!" said Santa.

Lock, Shock and Barrel started to pack Santa up again.

“Of course! That’s what I’m missing,” Jack said, as he whisked Santa’s hat from his head. Then he sent him on his way.

“This is worse than I thought. Much worse,” said Sally, watching as Lock, Shock and Barrel carried Sandy Claws away. Then she got an idea.

At their treehouse, Lock, Shock and Barrel tried to get Sandy Claws into the chute leading to Oogie Boogie's.

"I think he might be too big!" Shock said.

"No he's not. If he can go down a chimney he can fit down here!" Lock said thumping him with a plunger.

With a mighty shove, the trick or treaters squashed Sandy Claws into the pipe.

In Oogie's lair, the monster teased Sandy Claws as he lay on his roulette wheel. With no way to escape, Sandy begged Oogie to think of the children who were relying on him to deliver their gifts for Christmas morning, but Oogie refused to let him go.

Above, in the town square, people couldn't wait for Christmas to begin. Everyone that is, except Sally.

While nobody was looking Sally crept towards the fountain and emptied a bottle labelled 'Fog Juice' into the water, releasing a cloud of mist.
Sally slipped back into the crowd, as Jack emerged from his coffin sleigh.

"Think of us as you soar triumphantly through the sky," began the Mayor, wishing Jack farewell.
But the Mayor could not finish his speech. A fog had descended on the town, a fog so thick he could not even read the page in his hand.

"Oh no! We can't take off in this," said Jack in despair.
The crowd groaned.

Zero rushed to Jack's side. Jack tried to shoo him away, but then he noticed a light shining through the fog.

"My, what a brilliant nose you have," Jack said, looking at Zero's glowing snout. "The better to light my way." Jack sent Zero to the head of his skeleton reindeer and, before Sally could stop him, soared into the sky.

"Oh, how I hope my premonition is wrong," sighed Sally as she watched Jack leave.

Sally felt sure something very bad was going to happen to Jack, and that she and Jack would never find a way to be together.

High above the rooftops in the normal world, Jack flew into the night. He brought his sleigh down with a loud thump to deliver his first present.

"Santa!" cried a boy, woken from his sleep. The boy ran to see Santa, only to find Jack.

"And what did Santa bring you honey," the boy's mother asked, after Jack left.

His parents shrieked in terror, as the boy reached into the box and pulled out a shrunken head.

Jack flew, from house to house leaving ghastly gifts and screams in his wake.

Calls flooded the police station and news of the Santa imposter spread. The authorities advised people to lock their doors to keep Jack out.

From the surface of an enchanted cauldron, the citizens of Halloween Town watched as Jack skipped from chimney to chimney, leaving fear instead of laughter in his wake.

Then, they heard an announcement from a news reporter. "Reports are pouring in from all over the globe that an imposter is shamelessly impersonating Santa Claus, mocking and mangling this joyous holiday."

Jack's friends cheered. But one of Jack's friends was not cheering.

Sally listened in horror as the news reporter continued. “Police assure us that, at this moment, military units are mobilising to stop the perpetrator of this heinous crime.”

“Jack. Someone has to help Jack,” said Sally. “Where’d they take that Sandy Claws?”

Jack flew on, as military searchlights swept the sky. The searchlights were followed by the bright flashes and loud booms of exploding missiles.

“They’re celebrating! They’re thanking us for doing such a good job,” Jack cried, swerving to avoid a missile. “Whoa! Careful down there. You almost hit us,” Jack called.

Beneath Halloween Town, Sandy Claws hung from a hook in Oogie Boogie's lair, while the monster played a cruel dice game with his fate.

Oogie was about to roll the dice when he heard a noise behind him.

"My, my! What have we here?" Oogie ogled, when he saw a shapely leg poking into his lair.

As Oogie was distracted, a pair of hands slid down the rope to untie Sandy.

It was Sally. "I'll get you out of here," she whispered.

Oogie tickled the foot, but the leg came away in his hand. Oogie turned to see Sandy Claws escaping with Sally.

Consumed with rage, Oogie took a breath so deep it sucked Sandy and Sally from their ladder.

High above the normal world, Jack swerved to avoid the missiles.

"They're trying to hit us! Zero!" Jack warned, before a direct hit blew his sled to pieces.

In Halloween Town, Jack's friends watched as Jack fell from the sky.

"Terrible news, folks! The worst tragedy of our times," declared the Mayor as he drove throughout the town. "Jack has been blown to smithereens!"

In the normal world, the police announced their own terrible news, that there was no sign of the real Santa Claus, and Christmas would have to be cancelled.

Jack awoke, surrounded by the burned remains of his sleigh, wondering how he could have been so wrong. He'd wanted to do something wonderful. But he had tried to be something he wasn't.

Jack decided to go back to doing what he did best, being the pumpkin king, but first he threw open the doors to a grave and stepped inside, emerging into Halloween Town. Jack was determined to find Sandy Claws and save Christmas.

News of Jack's demise drifted down to Oogie's lair, where the monster had tied Sandy and Sally above a pit of hot lava.

"What's that you were saying about luck, ragdoll?" Oogie teased, rolling the dice. Oogie hoped for a high number which, according to his rules, would send Sally and Sandy into the flames.

But the game was rigged. Oogie slammed his fist on the table until the dice showed the number he wanted.

"Looks like I won the jackpot!" Oogie laughed. "Bye-bye doll face and sandman." He pulled a lever to send Sandy and Sally into the pit, but he didn't hear screaming. Oogie looked to see what went wrong, but they were gone.

“Hello Oogie,” Jack said, sitting in their place.

“Jack! But they said you were dead,” Oogie edged away.

Oogie stomped on a button that sent playing cards, wielding swords on Jack.

Jack escaped their slashing blades.

When Oogie saw that his attempts to thwart Jack weren't working, he hit yet another button, releasing a spinning saw from the roof.

"Jack, look out!" Sally cried as the blade swung toward Jack.

Jack leapt out of the way and landed face to face with Oogie.

But the monster had one more trick up his sleeve. "So long, Jack!" Oogie cackled, as he leaped onto a pendulum which lifted him away, leaving Jack alone on the wheel.

But Oogie's plan was about to unravel, and so was he.

"How dare you treat my friends so shamefully!" Jack boomed, grasping a loose thread hanging from Oogie. As Oogie rose into the air, Jack pulled on the thread. The monster's seams unravelled, releasing the bugs inside.

"Now look what you've done!" Oogie cried, now a writhing mass of creepy crawlies. He sobbed, as his insects crumbled into the fiery pit.

With Oogie defeated, Jack returned Sandy's hat.

"Forgive me, Mr. Claws. I'm afraid I've made a terrible mess of your holiday."

Sandy told Jack that the next time he wanted to take over a holiday, he should listen to Sally.

"I hope there's still time..." Jack said.

"To fix Christmas? Of course there is. I'm Santa Claus!" Sandy Claws replied, pinching his nose and flying into the sky.

"He'll fix things, Jack. He knows what to do," Sally said as they watched Sandy fly up the chute.

"How did you get down here, Sally?" Jack asked, looking at Sally as if he was seeing her for the very first time.

"Oh, I was trying to... Well, I wanted to... To..." Sally stuttered, unable to meet his gaze.

"To help me?" Jack said, placing a hand on her shoulder. "Sally, I can't believe I never realised that you..." But he didn't get to finish.

"Jack! Jack!" cried the Mayor, throwing down a rope. "Grab a hold, my boy!"

Jack grasped Sally's hand, as the Mayor and Lock, Shock and Barrel, pulled them to safety.

In the normal world, Santa sped through the skies, stopping at every house to replace Jack's gruesome gifts with presents made in Christmas Town.

"Good news, folks. Santa Claus, the one and only, has finally been spotted," a newscaster announced.

In Halloween Town, people rejoiced to see the return of their pumpkin king. And Jack was happy too.

"It's great to be home!" Jack proclaimed.

"Happy Halloween!" Santa cried from his sleigh in the sky, as he delivered a special gift to everyone in Halloween Town.

"Merry Christmas!" Jack called back as snowflakes filled the air.

Christmas had come to Halloween Town for the very first time.

Jack was happy that his friends finally understood the joy he had felt in Christmas Town. But Jack didn't join the fun. He still felt there was something missing, but this time Jack knew exactly what, or rather who, it was.

Jack searched the crowd for Sally and watched as she slipped away to walk alone.

He followed her to the snow-covered graveyard and asked to join her on top of the hill. Together at last, Jack took Sally's ragdoll hands in his as they kissed by the light of the moon.

# The End

# The Art of Tim Burton's The Nightmare Before Christmas

Following the completion of the short film *Vincent* in 1982, Tim Burton, who was employed at Walt Disney Feature Animation, wrote a three-page poem titled *The Nightmare Before Christmas*. Working with production designer Rick Heinrichs, Burton created concept art, storyboards and character models for the poem, which he shared with Disney animator Henry Selick. Burton left the studios in 1984, but often thought about the project. In 1990, Burton and Selick teamed up to create Skellington Productions and produce the story as a full-length stop motion film, with Selick directing. Joe Ranft was brought on as storyboard supervisor with Eric Leighton supervising the animation. Burton and Selick wanted the production design to resemble a pop-up book, with inspiration being drawn from sources including German Expressionism and Dr. Seuss. Production began in 1991, with 20 sound stages used for filming. A total of 109,440 frames were taken for the film, using 227 puppets. Jack Skellington had around 400 heads, allowing the puppet to express every possible emotion. Since its initial release, Tim Burton's *The Nightmare Before Christmas* has gone on to receive critical acclaim, with audiences praising the creativity of its visual storytelling and innovative use of stop-motion animation. Throughout this book you can see the concept art, story sketches and puppets from the following Skellington Productions artists.

## Tim Burton

Best known for directing gothic and dark fantasy films, American film director, producer, animator, writer and artist Tim Burton began his film career at the Walt Disney Animation Studios. Burton began making films at a young age and went on to study character animation at the California Institute of the Arts (CalArts). His student film *Stalk of the Celery Monster* earned him a place as an apprentice at Disney.

Burton's early career at Disney included animation work on films including *The Fox and the Hound* and *The Black Cauldron*. In 1982, Burton created a stop-motion animation for the studio: a black-and-white short tribute to Vincent Price, titled *Vincent*. It was in the same year that Burton penned a poem which he called *The Nightmare Before Christmas*. The poem was on its way to become a 30-minute TV special or a short film, but development halted, and Burton left Disney in 1984. Over the years Burton thought about the project and, in 1990, returned to produce the poem as a full-length stop-motion musical film in partnership with director Henry Selick.

Following the success of *The Nightmare Before Christmas*, Burton has gone on to collaborate with Disney on several projects, including the 1996 stop motion *James and the Giant Peach*, which features a cameo from Jack Skellington; the 2010 *Alice in Wonderland*; the 2016 sequel *Alice Through the Looking Glass*; and a 2019 live-action remake of Disney's *Dumbo*.
*Concept art on pages 2-3, 19, 29, 31, 45, 46, 59, 60, 63, 69* and *70-71*.
*Concept art likely to be by Tim Burton on pages 11, 13, 17, 18, 25, 38, 39, 41, 44, 49, 55* and *56*.

## Kendal Cronkhite

Kendal Cronkhite began her film career working on *The Nightmare Before Christmas* as assistant art director. In 1996, she worked with fellow art director Bill Boes on *James and the Giant Peach*, taking on the role of art director. In 1998, Cronkhite moved to the newly founded DreamWorks Animation Studios to art direct the movie *Antz*. She has since worked as a production designer on other DreamWorks films, including the *Madagascar* series and, most recently, *Trolls* and *Trolls World Tour*.
*Concept art on page 8, 16, 30, 36, 61, 67.*
*Concept art likely to be by Kendal Cronkhite on page 44.*

## Miguel Domingo

Miguel Domingo, also known as Michael Cachuela, studied at CalArts under both Joe Ranft for story and Chris Buck for animation. Domingo contributed to the 20th Century Fox film *Fern Gully*, released in 1992 as a storyboard artist before working with the Skellington Productions on *The Nightmare Before Christmas*. Domingo has since worked as a storyboard artist on Disney's *James and the Giant Peach* and Pixar's *The Incredibles* and *Ratatouille*.
*Story sketch on page 14.*

## Joe Ranft

Joe Ranft began studying in the character animation program at CalArts in 1978. His student film Good *Humour* was noticed by Disney executives, and he was offered a job at the studio. Ranft began his Disney career working on television projects, but his big break came when he moved to the Feature Animation department, working under Eric Larson. Ranft worked as a story artist, storyboard artist and storyboard supervisor on many Disney and Pixar films, and even lent his voice to characters in *The Brave Little Toaster*, *Toy Story* and *Cars*. For *The Nightmare Before Christmas*, Ranft took on the role of storyboard supervisor. Ranft tragically passed away in 2005, and his last film Cars was dedicated to his memory.
*Story sketches on pages 22 and 27.*
*Story sketches likely to be by Joe Ranft on pages 20 and 21.*

## Jørgen Klubien

Jørgen Klubien is an animation artist, writer and singer. Klubien has worked as a character animator and storyboard artist on a number of Disney films, including *Oliver & Company*, *The Little Mermaid*, *The Rescuers Down Under*, *A Bug's Life* and *Frankenweenie*. For *The Nightmare Before Christmas*, Klubein is credited with additional character design and also assisted with storyboards for the film. Klubien is also the lead singer of the Danish band Danseorkestret.
*Story sketches likely to be by Jørgen Klubien on pages 20 and 21.*

## Deane Taylor

Deane Taylor is a layout artist, writer, art director, production supervisor and director who has worked at Hanna-Barbera, Disney and MGM Animation. For *The Nightmare Before Christmas*, Taylor served as art director, and he also appeared in the documentary short *The Making of Tim Burton's The Nightmare Before Christmas*.
Concept art on *pages 30, 42 and 67.*

## Kelly Asbury

American film director, screenwriter, story supervisor, voice actor, animator, children's book author and illustrator, and non-fiction author, Kelly Asbury has worked on many animated films in many different roles. Asbury graduated from CalArts, where he studied animation and filmmaking. He joined Disney to work on *The Black Cauldron* as an in-between artist, and went on to work on films including *The Little Mermaid*, *Beauty and the Beast*, *Gnomeo and Juliet* and *Frozen*. Asbury worked as assistant art director on *The Nightmare Before Christmas*. Sadly, Asbury passed away in 2020 at the age of 60.
Concept art on *pages 33, 42 and 67.*

## Bill Boes

California native Bill Boes is a production designer, art director, model maker and special effects creator. Boes has worked across TV, live action, animation and stop-motion animation. For *The Nightmare Before Christmas*, Boes took on the role of assistant art director and also worked as a model maker. Boes also contributed to Disney's 1996 stop-motion film *James and the Giant Peach*.
Concept art on *page 51.*

**Concept art:** drawings, paintings or sketches prepared in the early stages of a film's development. Concept art is often used to inspire the staging, mood, and atmosphere of scenes.

**Production animation puppet:** a character, often created from cloth or foam latex, fabricated around an articulated armature, that is manipulated by an animator in small increments and photographed one frame of film at a time in order to give it the illusion of movement.

**Story sketch:** shows the action that's happening in a scene, as well as presenting the emotion of the story moment. Story sketches help visualise the film before expensive resources are committed to its production.